FOUL PLAY!

Ethan Flask and Professor von Offel's
Sports Science Match

MAD SCIENCE

by Kathy Burkett
Creative development by Gordon Korman

SCHOLASTIC INC.
New York Toronto London Auckland Sydney
Mexico City New Delhi Hong Kong

Table of Contents

Prologue

For more than 100 years, the Flasks, the town of Arcana's first family of science, have been methodically, precisely, safely, *scientifically* inventing all kinds of things.

For more than 100 years, the von Offels, Arcana's first family of sneaks, have been stealing those inventions.

Where the Flasks are brilliant, rational, and reliable, the von Offels are brilliant, reckless, and ruthless. The nearly fabulous Flasks could have earned themselves a major chapter in the history of science — but at every key moment, there always seemed to be a von Offel on the scene to "borrow" a science notebook, beat a Flask to the punch on a patent, or booby-trap an important experiment. Just take a look at the Flask family tree and then the von Offel clan. Coincidence? Or *evidence!*

Despite being tricked out of fame and fortune by the awful von Offels, the Flasks doggedly continued their scientific inquiries. The last of the family line,

Ethan Flask, is no exception. An outstanding sixth-grade science teacher, he's also conducting studies into animal intelligence and is competing for the Third Millennium Foundation's prestigious Vanguard Teacher Award. Unfortunately, the person who's evaluating Ethan for the award is none other than Professor John von Offel, a.k.a. the original mad scientist, Johannes von Offel.

Von Offel needs a Flask to help him regain the body he lost in an explosive experiment so many decades ago. He was nearly successful in *Out of This World! Ethan Flask and Professor von Offel Take On Space Science*. But unfortunately, the professor got a little *too* spaced out in his quest. And even worse, Prescott caught the whole misadventure on videotape!

So the lab assistants now have proof positive that the professor is a ghost. But they also realize they must keep von Offel's secret — or risk scuttling Mr. Flask's chances of winning the Vanguard Teacher Award. They even have to protect the professor's identity from their suspicious classmate, Max Hoof. And to top it all off, as Prescott, Luis, Alberta, and the rest of the sixth grade prepare for a soccer league championship, the professor is cooking up plans that could turn their team into a "von Awful" mess.

You'll find step-by-step instructions for the experiments mentioned on pages 8, 13, and 34 of this book in *Sports Science*, the Mad Science Experiments Log.

The Nearly Fabulous Flasks

Jedidiah Flask
2nd person to create rubber band

Augustus Flask
Developed telephone; got a busy signal

Oliver Flask
Missed appointment to patent new glue because he was mysteriously epoxied to his chair

Marlow Flask
Runner-up to Adolphus von Offel for Sir Isaac Newton Science Prize

Percy Flask
Lost notes on cure for common cold in pickpocketing incident

Mildred Flask Tachyon
Tranquilizer formula never registered; carriage horses fell asleep en route to patent office

Amaryllis Flask Lepton
Discovered new kind of amoeba; never published findings due to dysentery

Archibald Flask
Knocked out cold en route to patent superior baseball bat

Lane Tachyon
Developed laughing gas; was kept in hysterics while a burglar stole the formula

Norton Flask
Clubbed with an overcooked meat loaf and robbed of prototype microwave oven

Salome Flask Rhombus
Discovered cloud-salting with dry ice; never made it to patent office due to freak downpour

Constance Rhombus Ampère
Lost Marie Curie award to Beatrice O'Door; voted Miss Congeniality

Roland Flask
His new high-speed engine was believed to have powered the getaway car that stole his prototype

Michael Flask
Arrived with gas grill schematic only to find tailgate party outside patent office

Solomon Ampère
Bionic horse placed in Kentucky Derby after von Offel entry

Margaret Flask Geiger
Name was mysteriously deleted from registration papers for her undetectable correction fluid

Ethan Flask

The Awful von Offels

Johannes von Offel
Died creating the world's safest explosive

Wolfgang von Offel
Incinerated by
St. Elmo's Fire

Esmerelda von Offel Loch
Electrocuted by artificial
lightning bolt

Cameron Loch
Icebergologist on
the *Titanic*

Gustav von Offel
Killed by lava during
volcano study

Otto von Offel
Eaten during test of
shark repellent

Adolphus von Offel
Found lost continent
of Atlantis; never found
home again

Éduard von Offel
Died field-testing flawed
bulletproof vest

Sophia von Offel Kakos
Brained by falling
dinosaur bone

Professor John von Offel (?)

Rula von Offel Malle
Evaporated

Kurt von Offel
Weak batteries in antigravity backpack

Beatrice Malle O'Door
Drowned pursuing the Loch Ness Monster

Colin von Offel
Transplanted his brain into wildebeest

Felicity von Offel Day
Brained by diving bell during deep-sea exploration

Feldspar O'Door
Died of freezer burn during cryogenics experiment

Alan von Offel
Failed to survive field test of nonpoisonous arsenic

Johannes von Offel's
Book of Scientific Observations, 1891

Jedidiah Flask has organized the local children in a ball-kicking game. Flask no doubt brought this contest from his fancy college, along with its irritating reliance on "fair play" and "good sportsmanship." Not wanting our local youngsters to be led down the wrong path, I have outfitted a pair of child's shoes with a set of sharp metal spikes on each sole. Tomorrow, I will give these shoes — and a silver dollar — to the neighborhood bully. He, in return, has agreed to "step on some toes" during the next game. Others may only see his victims limping in body, but I will see them soaring in spirit as they grasp the true nature of competition. As I have demonstrated time and again, a contest is not won with hard work and honesty but with knavery and deceit. Oh, and often — as my bully friend would remind me — bribery.

CHAPTER 1

The Ailing Aces

As the bell rang for sixth-grade science, Luis Antilla limped through the lab door. Alberta Wong hobbled in behind him on crutches. Prescott Forrester followed, balancing a tall stack of schoolbooks.

Bringing up the rear was Professor von Offel. "Aren't students supposed to be in their seats *before* the bell rings?" he grumbled. His parrot, Atom, flew over the lab assistants' heads and landed on the brass perch on the professor's desk.

Prescott held Alberta's crutches as she lowered herself into her seat.

"Let's hear it for the Arcana Aces, soccer league finalists!" Mr. Flask began clapping, and the rest of the class joined in.

Alberta smiled weakly, but Luis frowned. "Big deal," he said. "There's no way we'll be in any shape for the championship next Saturday."

"As soccer coach, I have to disagree," Mr. Flask said. "We have a strong team that plays together well. Naturally, it doesn't help that both our goalie and our top scorer are injured, but we've overcome disadvantages before."

Luis raised his eyebrows. "Like what?"

Mr. Flask stroked his chin thoughtfully. "Well, we've played in the pouring rain quite a few times."

"Yeah, but each time our opponent was *also* playing in the pouring rain," Luis pointed out. "So it wasn't really a disadvantage."

"Point taken," Mr. Flask said. "Okay, let me rephrase that. We've triumphed over challenges before. After all, every game is a challenge. Now we just have a bigger challenge."

"Make that an *impossible* challenge," Prescott said. "The rest of us on the team are already working as hard as we can. We could practice every day this week and still not make up for losing Luis and Alberta."

"Practice every day this week?" Mr. Flask repeated. "Great suggestion. But we can't stop there. While you're right that we can't replace Luis and Alberta, we *can* bring in some fresh talent."

"From where?" Prescott asked.

"Hey," Sean Baxter said. "Look around! *I'd* make a great goalie. I was born to wear one of those cool, intimidating masks."

"You're thinking of a *hockey* goalie," Alberta said.

Sean laughed. "No kidding."

"I have a feeling Sean knows more about soccer than he's letting on," Mr. Flask said. "Sean, I'll see you at practice this afternoon. Anyone else?"

A few hands went up, including Max Hoof's. "Why should you lab assistants get all the glory?" he whispered to Alberta.

"Great! See you all at practice," Mr. Flask said. "Heather, we could use your help, too. What do you say?"

Heather Patterson looked puzzled. "Do they usually have cheerleaders at soccer games? I guess I could get a few of my friends together."

"A cheering section would be great," Mr. Flask said. "But I was hoping for more direct help. I suspect you might make a great forward."

"That's the position I played in second grade," Heather said. "But I haven't played for years. My mom said I could only do two sports, so I chose cheerleading and ballet."

"Both of which have been good practice for soccer," Mr. Flask said.

"How? There's no ball in either one!" Heather said.

"Certainly ball-handling is where I'd concentrate your practice this week," Mr. Flask said. "But there are other underlying skills in soccer, just as in any sport. There's a lot of running in soccer, which takes aerobic conditioning — a strong heart and lungs that allow you to exercise for a long time. You also need muscle strength and a good kinesthetic sense, or a feeling for where your body is and how it's moving. Both ballet and cheerleading allow you to develop all of these.

"A good forward also has to weave in and out of the opposing players," Mr. Flask continued. "That takes a good sense of dynamic balance. Heather, slip off your shoes and come to the front of the room."

Heather eased off her sneakers and stood up slowly. "Is this some kind of experiment?"

"Of course!" Mr. Flask motioned for her to come forward. "Now, are you right-footed or left-footed?"

Heather looked down at her sock-covered feet.

"It's easy, Heather," Sean said. "Which foot do you write your name with?"

Heather rolled her eyes.

Mr. Flask reached behind his desk and produced a soccer ball. He put it in front of Heather. "Kick it to Sean."

"I'd rather kick it *at* Sean."

Sean grinned. "Go for it. Like I said, I'm a natural goalie." He slid out of his chair and stood in the aisle, crouching slightly. "Let her rip!"

"Freeze!" Mr. Flask said. "Everyone look at how Sean is standing."

"I can't be breaking any soccer rules," Sean said. "I'm just bending my knees a little."

"Exactly," Mr. Flask agreed. "Any idea why?"

Sean looked down at his legs. "I don't know. It just feels right. I guess I'm bracing for the ball."

Mr. Flask nodded. "Without even thinking about it, you're getting yourself into a more stable — or better-balanced — position. That's an example of *static* balance, or being balanced when you're stand-

4

ing still. More on that in a moment. Okay, Heather, kick."

Heather slid her right toe under the ball and kicked. It popped up into the air; Sean had to jump high to catch it.

"Nice chip kick, Heather," Mr. Flask said. "And Sean, that was a nice save. If anyone ever asks, Heather, you're right-footed. Now, put your left foot on your right knee and your hands on your hips. Every five seconds, I'm going to say 'turn.' When I do, spin halfway around on the ball of your foot — that's the fleshy part right behind your toes. We're going to see how long you can keep it up without shifting your foot or hands."

Heather nodded.

"Okay, turn — turn —" Mr. Flask continued as Heather turned steadily.

"Nice job!" Mr. Flask said when she finally had to stop. "Not that it comes as a surprise to anyone who's seen you cheering or dancing. Both require a good sense of dynamic balance. Who else wants to try?"

A sea of hands shot up.

"Okay, everyone spread out."

Alberta raised her hand timidly.

Mr. Flask smiled at her. "Alberta and Luis are excused from this one." Then he noticed the professor standing up from his desk. "I have a feeling Professor von Offel is going to show us all how it's done," the teacher said.

The professor frowned. "I'm pretty spry for someone more than a hundred years old."

Prescott's jaw dropped. How had the professor let that slip? Alberta shot Luis a worried look. Max eyed the professor curiously.

Mr. Flask just laughed. "Apparently time hasn't dulled your sense of humor, either."

Prescott relaxed. Clearly, Mr. Flask thought the professor was joking.

"Everyone ready?" the teacher asked. "Now, turn — turn — turn —"

The classroom was filled with twisting, spinning bodies. Some students tipped over right away. Others spun with clockwork precision.

Max gave a few halfhearted turns, then stopped and watched the professor out of the corner of his eye. The older man's spins seemed weirdly effortless. Was it possible that his foot wasn't even touching the ground? And what was that red-and-blue blur behind him? Atom was doing the experiment, too! "Mr. Fla-ask! Mr. Fla-ask!" Max shouted out.

"What's wrong, Max?"

Max pointed over his shoulder. "Look!"

The teacher glanced behind Max, then knitted his eyebrows together. "What?"

Max looked back. The professor had returned to his chair and was busily writing with his quill. "I saw —" Max began. "And then —"

"Yes?" Mr. Flask encouraged.

"Oh, forget it," Max said. He flopped into his seat and crossed his arms.

The teacher gave him a puzzled smile. "Whatever it was, if you see it again, let me know."

Max grunted.

Mr. Flask faced the rest of the class. "So, back to balance. Any questions?"

"Why was that so hard?" Prescott glanced at Heather. "For me, that is."

"Keeping your balance is a matter of keeping your center of gravity over your base," Mr. Flask said. "Your base is the part of your body that touches the floor. So what was your base in the dynamic balance activity?"

Heather raised her hand. "The ball of my foot."

Mr. Flask nodded. "And your center of gravity is the point around which the weight of your body is balanced. Any idea where your center of gravity is?"

Luis looked down and pointed at a spot just below his navel. "Maybe here?"

"That's a good approximation," Mr. Flask said. "At least for when you're standing with your arms at your side." He reached into a desk drawer and pulled out a file folder. Then he used a pair of scissors to cut out a simple paper doll about 11 inches high.

"Hey, haven't I seen that guy on the door to the men's room?" Sean asked.

Mr. Flask laughed. "He does kind of look like a

men's room sign." He handed the figure to Luis. "How would you find this guy's center of gravity?"

Luis thought for a moment. "Well, you said that something's weight is balanced around its center of gravity. So maybe if I held the cardboard horizontally and balanced it on my finger, the place where my finger touched the cardboard would be its center of gravity."

"Try it," Mr. Flask said.

Luis shifted the cardboard figure around until it balanced on his fingertip.

"Mark that spot with a pen," the teacher said.

Luis did so, then held up the figure. "Hey, that spot is right around where the belly button would be."

Mr. Flask took the cardboard figure from Luis and bent its arms up. The doll's arms had been hanging by its sides. Now they were straight up, like someone reaching up to grab something off a high shelf. The teacher pressed both creases flat, then handed the figure to Alberta.

"Do you think his center of gravity has changed?" Mr. Flask asked.

Alberta thought. "His arms are higher, which means more weight up around his head. Seems like that would make his center of gravity go a little higher."

"Test your prediction," the teacher said.

Alberta balanced the figure on her fingertip and made a new mark. "Hey, it's definitely higher."

Mr. Flask took the figure and bent its arms back down. He handed it to Prescott. "Stand the doll up, and measure the distance from the tabletop to his original center of gravity."

Alberta rummaged in her backpack and handed Prescott a ruler. He held it up to the cardboard doll. "Five inches," he reported, and returned the figure to Mr. Flask.

Mr. Flask bent the upper leg and knee joints so that it looked like the figure was squatting. He held it up. "Sean's stable goalie stance, remember?" He handed the figure back to Prescott. "Now find his new center of gravity."

Prescott balanced the figure on his finger and made a new mark. Then he frowned. "Wait, you said that Sean was lowering his center of gravity. But my new mark is above Luis's original one, so his center of gravity is higher."

"Are you sure?" Mr. Flask said. "Stand the doll up, keeping its legs bent, and measure from the tabletop to the new center of gravity."

"Oh," Prescott said. He held up the ruler. "Wow, even though the center of gravity is higher on his body, it's lower to the ground."

"And closer to his feet, or base," Mr. Flask added.

"In fact, it's a half inch lower. That's a lot for such a little guy." Prescott handed the figure back to the teacher.

"I'll cut out some other cardboard shapes and

pass them around tomorrow," the teacher said. "We'll see if you can use your newfound skills to find the center of gravity for other shapes."

Prescott raised his hand. "I have another question about my center of gravity. It may shift around a little, but it seems like it's pretty much always over my feet. So what's the big deal?"

"Prescott, march up here and stand with your right foot, arm, and shoulder against the wall."

CHAPTER 2

Max on the Case

The color drained from Prescott's face. "But I didn't mean — I thought you *wanted* us to ask questions."

Mr. Flask laughed. "Of course. It's a scientist's number-one job. I'm just calling you up here for an experiment."

"Oh." Prescott walked up and stood with his right side to the wall.

"Feeling well balanced?" Mr. Flask said.

"I guess so," Prescott said. "I don't feel like I'm about to fall over or anything."

"You shouldn't," Mr. Flask affirmed. He pointed to Prescott's abdomen. "Right now your center of gravity is directly over your base. In this case, your base is made up of your two feet and, technically, the space between them. Does that sound like what your body is experiencing?"

Prescott nodded.

"That's all about to change," Mr. Flask said. "I'm going to ask you to lift your left foot. At that point, your center of gravity will still be in the middle of your body. But your base will shrink and shift. Suddenly, it will only be your right foot, which is naturally on the right side of your body. Let's see what happens. Lift that left foot."

Prescott got his foot four inches off the ground before he had to slam it back down again.

"Why did you put your foot down?" Mr. Flask asked.

"To keep from falling over!" Prescott said.

"I can't believe you can't do that!" Sean called out. "I bet I could."

"Come give it a try," Mr. Flask said.

Sean strode to the front of the room, swinging his arms like a muscle man. A minute later, he crept back to his seat like a mouse.

"Okay," he said. "I couldn't do it. What about Heather, then, if she's so good at balance?"

"Nobody could do that," Heather said. "I mean, I could do it *without* the wall, no sweat."

"How?" Mr. Flask asked.

Heather thought for a moment. "I guess my body would automatically lean a little to the right to put my center of gravity over my right foot." She gestured toward the wall. "But that's completely different. The wall would block me from shifting my center of gravity."

"That's exactly right!" Mr. Flask said. "In fact, I'm so confident no one can do this that I'll give an automatic A on the next test to anyone who can. Everyone hop up and try."

"But what's the next test going to be about?" Max asked.

"How about sports science?" The teacher grinned. "Clearly, there's enough interest here to begin a study unit on it. And it couldn't hurt you new soccer team members to learn a little more about the physics and physiology behind the game."

Soon the science lab was ringed with students — right shoulders, arms, and feet against the walls. Even the professor was trying the experiment, with Atom standing on his head.

Mr. Flask walked over to Luis and Alberta, hands hidden behind his back. "There are plenty of sports that don't require the use of legs." He produced six juggling balls with a flourish, then divvied them up between the two students. "Juggling is an excellent way to practice hand-eye coordination, an important part of a lot of sports. Why don't you two give it a try?"

Across the room, Sean planted himself behind Heather. "Psst. Can you lead us in a cheer to improve our performance?" he asked. "How about: 'Give me an A, give me an A, give me an A, give me an A! What have you got? A four-point-oh average.'"

Heather didn't even turn around. "I hate to break it to you, Sean, but you're not as funny as you think."

Max took a deep breath and crossed his fingers. He tried to lift his foot once, then twice. Each time, his foot left the ground for less than a second. "You've got to try again for the sake of your science grade!" he told himself. He pressed his body against the wall and jerked up his foot. This time, he kept it up for a second. He also nearly toppled over. When he regained his footing, he looked around the room. "Mr. Fla-ask," he whined. "This is imposs —" He stopped short. Over in the corner, the professor was calmly standing with his foot in the air. How was he doing it? Max left his spot and circled around behind the professor. He inched closer and closer, until suddenly Atom swung around to face him.

"Awk! Get lost!"

The professor reached up and snatched the bird off his head. He opened his mouth to speak to Atom, then noticed Max.

"Why were you spying on me?" the professor demanded. "Haven't you ever seen an old man before?"

"Well, not one who can stick his shoulder through a wall!"

The professor scowled. "You're a Hoof, aren't you?"

Max gulped. "Max Hoof."

"Your family has been in this town for a long time," the professor said.

Max nodded. "My great-great-great-great-great-great-grandfather Smedley Hoof was one of our founding fathers. I know because my mom is president of the Daughters of Arcana."

"Old 'Snake Oil' Smedley," the professor laughed. "He always did talk like he started this town. Truth was, he had no choice but to stay here. He'd been run out of three of our neighboring counties."

Max's eyes widened. "How did you know? My mother said never to talk about that!"

The professor ignored him. "I don't think people minded so much that Smedley was a cheat. I think the thing that really annoyed them was that he was such a whiner."

Max reddened. The professor just laughed and walked away.

"Time to head back to your seats," Mr. Flask announced. "Unless someone wants to come up here and show me they earned an A." When each seat was filled, the teacher smiled. "Once again, the laws of physics prove themselves unbeatable!"

Max eyed the professor, who calmly stared straight ahead.

After class, Max caught up with Prescott in the hallway. "Remember all that stuff you said about the professor being a ghost?"

Prescott's heart beat faster. "No! I mean, yes, I remember it. But it isn't true."

Max frowned. "Why do you say that?"

"Well, how *could* it be true?" Prescott said. "Whoever heard of a real ghost?"

"Then how do you explain the things the professor was doing in science class today?" Max said.

Prescott felt the color drain from his face. "What do you mean?"

"During the dynamic balance experiment, he was spinning like a top, and his feet weren't even touching the ground," Max said. "Then, he could actually do that impossible center of gravity experiment, but only because he was putting his shoulder *through* the wall!"

"Look, I was wrong about the professor," Prescott blurted out. "Whatever you think you saw, just forget about it."

Max shook his head. "No way. I'm going to prove the professor is a ghost. When I do, I bet I make lab assistant."

Glancing ahead, Prescott saw Professor von Offel in front of his office door. Atom was perched on his shoulder, busily preening some wing feathers. The professor tried to turn the knob, but the door was locked. He patted his pockets for keys but came up empty. So he boldly strode forward — right toward the locked door!

Prescott grabbed Max by the arm and whirled him around. He heard a squawk and a thump behind him.

"What?" said Max. "Our next class is the other way."

"All this talk of ghosts has made me thirsty," Prescott said, spying the water fountain. He pulled Max toward it. "If you want to keep talking to me, you'll have to come, too."

"No, I've said my piece." Max turned back. "Hey, the professor left his bird in the hall. It looks stunned or something."

Prescott spun around in time to see the professor's door inch open. A hand reached out, grabbed Atom by the claws, and yanked the parrot inside.

"You know, I think there's something weird about that bird, too," Max said, walking away.

Prescott paused, then knocked on the professor's office door. A moment later, von Offel answered. When he recognized Prescott, his frown turned into a nasty grin. "It's my little spirit-chasing friend," he said.

"Look, *I* know you're a ghost," Prescott began. "And you know that I know you're a ghost. And I know that you know that I know you're a ghost —"

The professor laughed. "So have you shown young Flask your 'moving pictures' of me covered with baking flour?"

Prescott squirmed uncomfortably. "Actually, I've decided to keep my video evidence a secret — for now, at least. But you've got to do your part, too. Max Hoof is starting to suspect you, and you just sailed through your office door not 10 feet away from him! I had to think fast to keep him from seeing you."

The professor's smile broadened. "Having you learn my secret was the most liberating thing that has ever happened to me. Now I see that no matter what evidence the adults here behold, they're un-

17

likely to believe it. As for you children — well, who would take *your* word for anything? And I've realized, as clearly you have, too, that it's in everyone's best interest at Einstein Elementary to conceal my true identity. Good afternoon!" He cheerfully shut the door between them.

"But —" Prescott said.

The professor stuck his face right through the door. "Yes?"

Prescott stared at the professor's head, which looked like a hunting trophy hanging on the door.

"Are you crazy?" Prescott said. He looked nervously from side to side.

"This is what you wanted, isn't it, when you started trying to prove I was a ghost?" The professor laughed. "Listen, young man. I'm finished with sneaking around."

"But you can't —" Prescott stopped, hearing voices in the next corridor. "Someone's coming! Get back in there!"

The professor laughed nastily and faded away.

After soccer practice, Prescott raced to Alberta's house, where she and Luis were elevating their injuries.

"We've got a problem!" Prescott said.

"The championship?" Luis scoffed. "It's a lost cause. No offense, but even with the Aces in tip-top shape, we'd have a hard time against the Strikers.

They're a good team, with a reputation for playing tough."

Alberta sighed. "It's nice of Mr. Flask to try to win one for us, but —"

"Actually, I meant the professor," Prescott said. "Remember how we realized that if we expose him, Mr. Flask will lose the Vanguard Teacher Award? Well, the professor has figured it out, too."

"Thus, the little slip about being more than a hundred years old?" Luis said.

Prescott nodded. "That's not all. Max was watching the professor during our balance experiments. He noticed that the professor's feet don't completely touch the ground, and he saw him put his shoulder through a wall. I told him he must have imagined everything. But he said he's going to do whatever it takes to prove that the professor is a ghost."

"Think of all the things you tried before you got some real evidence on the professor," Luis said. "He'll probably never get any."

"Maybe," Alberta said. "But Max can be like a pebble in your shoe — a small but steady nuisance that you try to ignore, but then suddenly —"

"You want to dump him onto the ground?" Prescott said.

"I was going to say that suddenly you have no choice but to pay attention to him," Alberta said. "So if Max bugs Mr. Flask long and hard enough, Mr. Flask may have to listen."

"Especially if the professor keeps being so reckless," Prescott said. "What are we going to do?"

Luis thought for a moment. "Let's play this like a soccer game. The professor is some crazy halfback, kicking the ball all over the field. Max is a forward, looking for any chance to take control of the ball and kick it into the goal. We all have to be goalies, blocking his every shot."

CHAPTER 3

Putting Traction into Action

Max hobbled into the science lab. "Mr. Fla-ask!" he said. "My soccer career is over before it even began."

"How did you get injured?" Mr. Flask asked. "I thought all the new players took an easy practice yesterday."

"It's these cleats," Max moaned. "My mom said I had to break them in before the game. But they're so uncomfortable. And I've slipped and fallen about 20 times! I thought these things were supposed to give you a better grip."

Luis made a face. "They do, Max, but on soft grassy fields, not hard classroom floors!"

Max lifted up one of his soccer shoes and exposed a sole covered with plastic knobs. "But in soft soil, these cleats would sink into the ground."

"That's exactly the point!" Alberta said.

Mr. Flask clasped his hand on Max's shoulder. "You're a walking science experiment today." He turned toward the class. "Today, we're going to follow

Max's lead! Everyone outside to investigate sports shoes and playing surfaces."

The bell rang. The professor, ready to coast through the door, was stopped short by a stream of exiting sixth graders.

"What's all this, Flask?" he demanded. "Giving up on class today before it even begins?"

Mr. Flask laughed. "We're just headed out to the soccer field, Professor."

"Hey," Sean said. "That makes this a real 'field trip'!"

Five minutes later, Mr. Flask was leading the group across the soccer field.

Max stepped confidently along. "You're right, Mr. Flask. This grass is 10 times better than the linoleum floors at school."

"The cleats on the bottom of your soccer shoes can get a good grip on this grass," Mr. Flask said. "Scientists would say you have good *traction*. Now, when you use your legs to push back, your body is propelled forward. Back on the smooth floor, the hard plastic cleats couldn't get any traction. When you pushed back, your leg slid back and you lost your balance."

"My center of gravity was no longer over my base," Max said.

"Exactly." The teacher grinned. "Now let's try another surface." He led them down a slightly muddy path.

Alberta stopped short. "I don't think I can go any farther on these crutches. They're sinking in."

Mr. Flask motioned for Alberta to take a higher, drier route.

"Max, are you still getting good traction?" Mr. Flask asked.

"Not as good as on the grass," Max said. "But still better than in the building."

"A lot of players have a second set of soccer shoes with longer cleats on them," Mr. Flask said. "Longer cleats give them better traction in mud."

"Well, I for one am getting no traction," Heather said. "This mud is slippery."

"If you were getting *no* traction, you wouldn't be moving at all," Sean said.

"You know what I meant," Heather snapped.

"Let's see your soles," Mr. Flask said.

Heather lifted up her foot. "They're pretty flat," she said. "I guess there's nothing there to grip the soil."

Mr. Flask nodded. He looked around at everyone's feet. "Most of you are wearing sneakers. The ridges on the bottom, called *treads*, help your shoes grip grass and soil, though not as well as cleats do."

Max looked at the bottom of his soccer shoes. "Ugh! How am I going to get the mud off my new cleats? My mom is going to kill me!"

"Everyone head to the building and wipe your feet on the mat at the back door," Mr. Flask said. "Then meet me over at the playground slide."

Most of the class took off for the building, but Max stayed with Mr. Flask. Prescott dropped back, too, so that he could eavesdrop.

"You know how scientists are supposed to be observant?" Max said to the teacher.

Mr. Flask nodded.

"Well, I just observed that everyone has muddy feet except for two people," Max said. "Alberta doesn't, because she couldn't go through the mud with her crutches. But the professor also doesn't."

The teacher shrugged. "He probably avoided the mud. Not every grown-up is as willing to get dirty as I am."

"But he was standing right next to me," Max said.

"No, that was me!"

Mr. Flask and Max turned to look at Prescott.

"You think I can't tell the difference between you and the professor?" Max said to Prescott.

"You think *I* can't?" Prescott retorted. "If I say it was me, then it was me."

"It was definitely the professor," Max insisted. "Unless you were wearing a fuzzy gray wig and a monocle."

"I think I saw the professor up with Alberta." Prescott turned back toward his friend, who was hopping behind. "Hey, Alberta! The professor was standing with you, right?"

Alberta looked confused.

"Therefore," Prescott continued, "it's no big mystery that he didn't get mud on his shoes."

"Oh, right," Alberta said. "Yeah, the professor was definitely with me, up on dry ground the whole time."

Mr. Flask looked from Alberta to Prescott to Max. "This is all very interesting," he said finally. "But we have some science to do. Prescott, could you run back to class and bring Hector and Hip-Hop? Also, a carrot and a magnifying lens."

Prescott nodded and took off.

"What do a gecko and a rabbit have to do with sports science?" Max asked.

Mr. Flask smiled. "Do you think we're the only animals who need to get a grip?"

A few minutes later, the whole class was gathered around the metal slide in the center of the playground. Mr. Flask stood at the top. "I'm here to announce a new Olympic sport called the Ultimate Slide Climb, in which contestants race to the top of a 100-foot metal slide. Your task is to decide what kind of shoes the Slide Climb athletes should wear. To aid in your decision, you may experiment with this eight-foot practice slide."

Max looked at the slide's steep slope and smooth surface. "Definitely not cleats," he said. "If they can't get traction on smooth linoleum floors, then they can't get traction on this metal surface, either."

"Want to test your prediction — very carefully?" Mr. Flask said.

Max stepped up onto the horizontal base of the slide and grabbed the side rails. He took a cautious step and immediately slid back down.

"Okay, the Slide Climb Commission rules: no cleats," Mr. Flask said. "What other kind of shoe should we consider?"

"Not mine," Heather said. "They're too smooth on the bottom."

"Those look like leather soles," Mr. Flask said. "Why don't you give them a try?"

Heather stepped up on the slide base and tried to get a footing on the slope. She shook her head and hopped off.

Alberta raised her hand. "I've noticed that the rubber on the bottom of my crutches grips surfaces really well. It's a good thing, too, because I have to lean on them when I'm going up or down hills."

"I think the Slide Climb Commission has to forbid crutches for safety's sake," Mr. Flask said. "But maybe it would consider shoes with the same material on the bottom."

"Sneakers!" Prescott said. "They have rubber soles."

Mr. Flask gestured toward the bottom of the slide. "Perhaps you could give us a demonstration?"

Prescott stepped carefully onto the horizontal base, grasped the side rails, and worked his way to the top. Mr. Flask gave him a high five.

"Sneakers look like a promising shoe for this athletic event," the teacher said. "But can you explain the scientific principle behind them?"

Prescott looked at the bottom of his sneaker. "Well, they have treads, which can grip stuff." He pointed at the slide's smooth surface. "But there's nothing there for them to grip, so that can't be it."

"It may seem like there's nothing there to grip," Mr. Flask said. "But if you looked at the surface under a very powerful microscope, you'd see all kinds of little ridges and valleys."

"The rubber must grip them," Alberta said. "But how?"

"What are some of rubber's characteristics?" Mr. Flask said.

"Well, it's kind of soft," Alberta said. "If you push on it, it molds around your finger a little."

"Hey, maybe the rubber can mold around those microscopic ridges, too," Prescott said. "That would give it some grip."

Mr. Flask nodded. "Sounds like traction in action, a simplified version, of course. Okay, now let's check in with the animal kingdom to see how they deal with traction. Prescott, could you bring out Hip-Hop?"

Prescott coasted down the slide and undid the clasp on a small cage. He slid out a caramel-colored rabbit and held her carefully, with one hand under her shoulders and the other under her tail.

Atom's eyes flashed. "Fresh rabbit meat. It's about time!" He launched himself from the professor's shoulder and circled lazily overhead.

"When do rabbits need good traction?" Mr. Flask asked.

Alberta looked up at Atom. "How about when they're running away from predators?"

"Awk, awk, awk!" Atom chortled.

"Exactly right, Alberta," Mr. Flask said. "Rabbits have a lot of natural predators."

Sean pointed up at Atom. "And some unnatural ones, too."

Prescott cradled the rabbit to his chest. "She's really struggling. I think Atom's making her nervous."

Atom broke off circling and headed straight toward Prescott and Hip-Hop. Prescott ducked and held the rabbit even closer.

"Professor von Offel, I'm sure Atom's behavior is completely natural," Mr. Flask began.

"Of course, it's natural!" the professor said. "Why on earth wouldn't it be?"

"It's also natural that it makes Hip-Hop nervous," Mr. Flask continued. "So I wonder whether you could call Atom down until we finish this activity and get our animals back into the classroom."

"Of course, I can call him down!" the professor said. "What makes you think I couldn't?" He held up his finger like a perch. "Down, Atom!"

Atom kept circling. "Awk, awk, awk," he chuckled.

The professor scowled. He removed the monocle from his eye, twirled it by the chain for a few seconds, and then launched it skyward. It neatly wrapped itself around Atom's claw. The professor reeled the bird in and shoved him into his front coat pocket. Then von Offel turned to the teacher. "Carry on, Flask."

CHAPTER 4

The Professor at Play

Atom backed himself out of the professor's pocket and clawed his way up to von Offel's shoulder. He swayed a little but was able to keep his footing.

"Is Atom okay?" Mr. Flask asked.

"Don't worry," the professor said. "And don't dilly-dally, either. Let's get on with your little competition."

Mr. Flask turned to his class. "Okay, back to rabbits. What kinds of surfaces do they run on?"

Luis raised his hand. "Mostly grass and dirt."

"Hey, the same surfaces that my cleats are good for!" Max said.

"Good observation," Mr. Flask said. "Prescott, gently lift Hip-Hop's back paw so that everyone can see it. Does it have anything in common with cleats?"

"The claws," Heather said. "They're like cleats because they can get a grip on grass and soil. They're also different, though, because they don't cover the whole bottom of her foot."

Mr. Flask nodded. "How well do you think Hip-Hop would do in the Ultimate Slide Climb?"

"If those claws are anything like my cleats, not too well," Max said.

Mr. Flask took the rabbit from Prescott and put her on the slide's horizontal base. "Could you bring over a carrot, Prescott?"

Mr. Flask held the carrot halfway up the slide. Hip-Hop balanced on her back feet and sniffed the air. She took a few cautious hops toward the carrot and stopped to sniff again. Then she tried to scramble up the slope, her claws scratching uselessly on the polished metal.

After a moment, Mr. Flask lowered the carrot into reach. "You get an A for effort," he said. Hip-Hop stopped scrambling and happily munched her prize.

Mr. Flask lifted up a small aquarium. Inside, a green lizard about the length of his hand clung to one of the glass sides. "Now, can anyone tell me when a day gecko like Hector needs traction?" He glanced over at Atom. "*Besides* when it might need to escape a predator."

"Day geckos eat insects," Luis said. "So they'd need to be able to climb trees to find them."

"And not just trees," Alberta said. "Look how easily Hector clings to the side of his aquarium. Maybe wild day geckos have to climb smooth leaves or rocks. How does he do that, anyway?" She leaned in for a closer look at Hector's feet. "Hey! the bottoms of Hector's feet look like sneaker treads."

"Nice comparison," Mr. Flask said. "Those ridges do look like sneaker treads, though scientists don't think they function like treads. Maybe you could research that when you grow up.

Luis frowned. "Anyway, we already said that it wasn't the sneaker treads that helped Prescott climb up the ladder. It was the rubber soles gripping all of the microscopic ridges. But Hector's feet aren't made of rubber. So what grips?"

Mr. Flask smiled. "If you look at Hector's toes under a powerful microscope, you'll see that those treads are made up of tiny *bristles*."

"Like toothbrush bristles?" Sean laughed.

"Basically," the teacher said. "But at the end of each bristle is a cluster of spatula-shaped structures. And here's where it gets really cool. Those little tips actually bond with a surface on the molecular level. That is, the individual molecules in the gecko's toes stick to the individual molecules of the climbing surface."

"No wonder geckos can climb on the ceiling," Luis said. "That's way beyond what even the fanciest sneakers can do. But wouldn't it be cool to have shoes that worked like gecko feet?"

Mr. Flask nodded. "The scientists who are studying gecko feet think so, too. Right now, they're concentrating on designing robots that can climb like geckos. But they've also thought about making tennis shoes that could give us that capability."

"You need tons of traction for rock-climbing," Alberta said. "It would be great to have gecko shoes and gloves."

"And wouldn't it be amazing to play a basketball game where you could climb the walls or even the ceiling?" Prescott said. "Maybe on the space station or something."

"Great ideas!" Mr. Flask said. "Now, let's see if Hector can show us whether gecko shoes would work for the Ultimate Slide Climb." He pulled Hector out of his habitat and placed him at the bottom of the slope. "Conveniently for us, day geckos naturally move up to get away from 'danger'." As the teacher spoke, the gecko quickly scampered up the smooth slide.

"We have a winner," Luis said.

Mr. Flask carried Hector's habitat to the top of the slide and coaxed him back inside.

Atom, still swaying on the professor's shoulder, sighed. "Guess I'll have to eat lunch later."

As Mr. Flask led the class inside, the professor lagged behind. He watched the class disappear through the doorway, then stepped up on the slide's horizontal base.

"What are you doing, Johannes?" Atom said. "Recess was over for you a long time ago."

"True, it's been more than a century since I played on a sliding board," the professor said. "But I'm not the same person I used to be. To be specific, I'm only 65 percent of that person. Who knows what I can do in my semicorporeal state?" He placed a foot on the slope and stepped easily up the slide.

Atom looked down at the smooth slope. "How did you get enough traction to do that? Your feet don't even touch the ground!"

The professor launched himself down the slide like an Olympic skier. "One of the best things about my current physical state is that I don't have to play by any rules — not even the rules of physics." He stopped abruptly at the bottom, then started to slide back *up* the slope.

"Don't you care about getting caught?" Atom pointed one wing at the school. "Look!"

The professor glanced over at the building. He looked completely uninterested. "What?"

Inside, Prescott was trying to pry Max away from the hallway window.

"He just slid *up* the slide!" Max said. "Mr. Flask has got to see this." He picked his way down the hall, cleats clicking on the smooth floor.

Prescott hurried after him. "What was there to see? The professor was just walking up the slide. All that proves is that he has rubber soles."

"Don't pretend you didn't see him *sliding* up," Max said. "If your observation skills are that poor, you have no business being a lab assistant."

Prescott thought for a moment. "Did you ever consider that maybe you need to have your glasses prescription checked?"

"For your information, my mother takes me to have it checked twice a year." Max stepped into the classroom. "Mr. Flask!" he shouted. "Look out on the playground, quick!"

"Did we leave someone behind?" The teacher rushed to the window, a roll of quarters in his hand. He surveyed the empty yard.

"Isn't the professor still doing his crazy tricks out there?" Max asked.

"Awk! Awk! Awk!"

Max turned to see the professor stride calmly through the door. "What are you doing here?"

The professor fixed him with a stare. "Evaluating your teacher for the Vanguard Teacher Award, of course. Don't you pay attention to anything your teacher says? That won't look very good in my report."

Max crossed his arms and hobbled back to his seat. His cleats click-clacked across the floor.

Mr. Flask watched Max thoughtfully. He opened his mouth to speak.

Prescott's hand shot into the air. "Mr. Flask, are we going to experiment with those?"

The teacher looked down at the quarters in his hand. "Yes, I thought we had just enough time left to experiment with projectile motion."

Prescott stood up and held out his hand. "Would you like me to pass them out?"

Mr. Flask handed over the roll. "Two quarters per lab group," he said. "Everyone place one coin at the edge of the table, with almost half of it hanging over. Place the other coin a few inches away. One person flicks the second coin at the first, trying to hit it off center. The other lab partners watch the coins and listen for the sound of them hitting the ground."

When Prescott reached the end of the first row, he stopped at the professor's desk. "You've got to be more careful," he whispered. "I can't go on saving you like this!"

The professor just grinned. "You will if you want your precious Mr. Flask to win his little award."

At soccer practice that afternoon, Mr. Flask paired each new player with an experienced player for some one-on-one drills.

Prescott passed Max a practice ball. "You dribble first, and I'll go for the tackle."

Max's eyes grew wide. "Tackle? But this isn't football."

Prescott shook his head impatiently. "Didn't you read your team handbook? Tackling just means taking the ball away from someone."

"Oh, yeah," Max said. He scooped up the ball and got into position about 20 feet away. As Max dribbled the ball toward an imaginary goal, Prescott moved into his path. Max swerved toward Prescott's right.

"It's too obvious that you're going to try to pass on my right side," Prescott said. "Try to keep me guessing."

"You just *think* I'm obvious!" Max got about a yard away from Prescott, then made a sharp turn and tried to circle around Prescott's left. Prescott snapped out his left foot and booted the ball away.

"Okay, my turn on offense." Prescott chased after the ball and trapped it. He dribbled straight for Max, faked left, then turned right, leaving Max spinning.

"That's not fair!" Max said. "I wasn't ready!"

"Do you think the Strikers are going to wait until you're ready?" Prescott lobbed the ball to Max.

Max caught it like a basketball.

"You're not the goalie, Max!" Prescott said. "Never touch the ball with your hands. If you do that during the championship, the Strikers will get a direct free kick. That one dumb move could lose us the game."

"What's the big deal?" Max snapped. "This is just practice."

"Is there a problem here?" Mr. Flask jogged across the field toward them. He came to a stop in front of Prescott. "Whatever's going on between you two, I need you to solve it off the soccer field. Right here, we're a team, and we have to act that way. Prescott, I'm sure Max is interested in your pointers."

"Hmmph," Max sniffed.

"But I'm also sure you can find a more appropriate way to deliver them."

Prescott nodded reluctantly.

"Okay, let's see some more drills," Mr. Flask said, trotting away.

CHAPTER 5

All Eyes on the Ball

Heather walked purposefully up to Mr. Flask, a soccer ball under her arm. "I'm not a quitter," she said. "But I think you'd better find another forward."

Prescott was holding Alberta's crutches as she slid into her desk. "But you look great, Heather!" he said, and immediately started blushing.

Alberta rolled her eyes. Luis tried to hide a smile.

"What I mean is, you've been playing so well in practice," Prescott said. "You can't abandon the team now."

Heather frowned. "You wouldn't miss me. Since tomorrow's the big game, I dug out my old soccer ball and brought it to school. I figured I could fit in extra practice between classes and during lunch. But I've completely lost my touch. Watch." She dropped her ball and gave it a sharp kick. It skipped weakly across the science lab floor.

Mr. Flask scooped up the ball and pressed it between his palms. "You haven't lost your touch, Heather. You've just lost some air."

The bell rang. Professor von Offel breezed into the lab with Atom on his shoulder. Max slipped in a second later, clearly tailing the pair. He watched the professor sit down, then headed for his own desk. As he passed Prescott, he whispered, "He was just out on the swing set."

"So?" Prescott said.

"See for yourself," Max replied.

Prescott looked out the window at the playground. The swing was wound tightly around the pole at the top.

"He was *on* the swing when he did that," Max said.

Prescott gulped. "Did anyone else see it?"

Max shook his head. "I didn't have time to get Mr. Flask."

"I guess it's just as well," Prescott said.

"What do you mean?"

Prescott avoided Max's gaze. "You wouldn't want Mr. Flask to know you're hallucinating. He might even think you're lying."

Max made a face. "Who's lying now?"

At the front of the classroom, Mr. Flask cleared his throat. "Please take your seats so we can start class."

Max crossed his arms and stomped down the aisle.

Mr. Flask tossed Heather's soccer ball into the air. "Another very important piece of sports equipment has been brought to my attention. Can anyone tell me what attributes, or characteristics, a soccer ball should have?"

Luis raised his hand. "Well, it has to be round, so it can roll."

Mr. Flask picked up a piece of chalk and wrote, SHAPE = SPHERE. He turned back to the class. "What else?"

Alberta thought for a moment, then raised her hand. "A soccer ball also needs to have just the right weight. If it were as heavy as a bowling ball, it would take too much effort to kick it, and it would hurt. On the other hand, if it were as light as a balloon, I don't think it would go very far. It just wouldn't have enough, well, oomph."

Mr. Flask laughed. "Very good point, Alberta. Scientists call that oomph *momentum*, and it's partly dependent on an object's weight. To understand why momentum is important for a sports ball, you first have to think about conditions off the playing field — way off the playing field, in outer space. If you traveled beyond our solar system and threw or kicked a ball, it would travel in a straight line and at a constant speed."

Luis's eyebrows shot up. "Forever?" he asked.

"Well, until something stopped it or made it change directions," the teacher replied. "As we learned before, space is pretty empty. So that ball could be flying along at the same speed for millions of years."

Sean thrust both hands into the air, as if blocking a goal. "Not with Space Goalie Sean on the job."

Mr. Flask laughed. "Now, you may have noticed that it doesn't work the same way on Earth, or more precisely, in Earth's atmosphere," he continued. "On Earth, that ball would slow down pretty quickly because of *air resistance*, or friction between the ball and the air. Here's where Alberta's oomph comes in: Momentum helps a ball overcome air resistance. That is, the more momentum a ball has, the longer it takes for air to stop it, and so the farther it travels. For example, a flying baseball has a lot of momentum. It can travel pretty far through the air and still hit your mitt hard when you catch it. A flying Wiffle Ball, on the other hand, has very little momentum. Air slows it down quickly. So, it can't travel nearly as far, and it doesn't hit your mitt with nearly as much force."

Mr. Flask added to the board, *Weight = just right (between 14 and 16 oz.)*. He turned back to the class. "Anything else?"

Prescott raised his hand. "Well, soccer balls are usually black and white, but I don't think color is that important."

"Oh, yeah?" Sean called out. "I'd like to see you play with a green soccer ball."

"Show him a soccer field covered with red astroturf and he could," Luis said.

Mr. Flask smiled. "Here's what I think you're both

getting at." He wrote on the board, *Color = must be easily visible against playing field.*

"Mr. Fla-ask," Max said. "There shouldn't be anything else that could throw you off, either. Like, what if your opponent showed up with a ball that was smaller than you were used to? You might try to kick it and miss. That won't happen tomorrow, right?"

"Don't worry, Max," the teacher said. He wrote on the board, *Size = 27–28 inches in circumference, or distance around the middle.*

"And I've been practicing with a leather ball," Max continued. "Can they show up with a ball made of something weird, like" — he looked around the classroom — "wood? Or metal? Or parrot feathers?"

Atom squawked indignantly.

"Our league has rules about that, too," Mr. Flask said. He wrote, *Material = leather or suitable plastic.* He looked around at the class. "What else does a soccer ball need?"

The sixth graders were silent. Alberta looked at Luis and shrugged. Mr. Flask held Heather's ball at shoulder height and let it go. It fell, bounced a puny eight inches into the air, then one, then skittered to a stop.

"Oh, not enough air!" Heather called out.

Mr. Flask gave her a thumbs-up sign, then reached behind his desk and pulled out a bicycle pump. He fished around in his top drawer for a ball adapter and screwed it onto the pump. Then he inserted the needle into the ball and worked the pump handle for half a minute. When he was done, he dropped the ball from shoulder height again. This time it rebounded a full yard into the air, then bounced 10 more times before coming to rest at the teacher's feet.

He turned and wrote on the board: *Inflation = enough air so that when ball is dropped from 100 inches onto a hard surface, it rebounds to a height between 60 and 65 inches.*

Then he passed the ball to Heather, who dribbled it deftly up the aisle. "I'm back!" she said. "Count me in for tomorrow's game." She gave the ball a gentle chip kick, then watched it bounce. "So how did that extra air make my ball so much bouncier?"

Mr. Flask reached into his drawer and pulled out a rubber pinky ball, a spongy pink ball the size of a tennis ball. He placed it on the floor. "Let's start by talking about how a ball bounces," he said. "Prescott, come up here and help me."

Prescott nodded and walked over to the ball.

"Okay, give this ball potential energy," Mr. Flask said.

Prescott raised his eyebrows.

"What I mean is, pick it up," the teacher said.

Prescott bent down for the ball.

"When the ball was on the floor, it essentially had

no energy," Mr. Flask said. "We could have watched it for a million years, and it never would have moved on its own. When Prescott lifted the ball off the floor, the story changed. Now, the ball has *potential energy*, energy that could be used to make it move in the future."

Sean laughed. "Yeah, like if he drops it."

"Exactly!" Mr. Flask said. "And I *am* going to ask him to drop it in a moment. When he does, that potential energy will turn to *kinetic energy*, or energy in motion. Now, here's a tricky question: What do you think will happen to that energy when the ball hits the floor and stops moving?"

"Well, the ball won't really stop moving, will it?" Luis said. "It'll just change directions after it bounces."

"Actually, it *will* stop moving for a split second just before it changes directions," Mr. Flask said.

"Oh, at the very bottom of the bounce," Luis said.

Mr. Flask nodded. "So where will that energy be during that split second?"

Luis thought. "Energy can't be created or destroyed, right?"

Mr. Flask smiled. "That may be the most fundamental law of our universe."

Alberta raised her hand. "The energy can change forms, though. Like from potential energy to kinetic energy."

"Yep, and back again," Mr. Flask said.

"So does the ball's kinetic energy somehow change back to potential energy during that split second?" Luis asked.

Mr. Flask reached back into the drawer and pulled out a second rubber pinky ball. He pushed it hard onto the surface of his desk. "See how the bottom of this ball is compressed, or flattened? That's what happens when the ball makes contact with the floor. The rubber compresses, and the kinetic energy becomes potential energy stored in that compressed part of the ball."

"Huh?" Sean said.

"Here's an easier way to visualize it," Mr. Flask said. "Imagine that instead of pushing a rubber ball into this table, I'm pushing a metal spring. That compressed spring would be full of potential energy."

"That is easier," Sean agreed.

"When I let go," the teacher continued, "the potential energy would turn to kinetic energy, meaning that the spring would pop up like a jack-in-the-box."

Sean nodded.

"The same thing happens with a bouncing ball." He held the ball in his hand and moved it down toward the table. "Kinetic energy — energy in motion." The ball touched the surface of the table. He pushed the ball so that the bottom compressed. "Kinetic energy changing into potential energy." He eased the pressure on the ball so that it returned to its original shape. "Potential energy changing back into kinetic energy." He lifted the ball off the table. "Kinetic energy again, but in the opposite direction."

"Wow," Luis said.

"Okay, Prescott, give it a try," Mr. Flask said.

Prescott dropped the ball, watched it bounce, then caught it again. "I never really thought about bouncing before, but it's pretty cool to know what's going on."

"Yeah," Heather said. "But how does this fit in with the air inside my soccer ball?"

Mr. Flask pushed the pinky ball onto the table's surface again. "With this ball, it's the rubber that compresses and stores the potential energy," he said. "With a properly inflated soccer ball, it's the air inside that compresses. And as it turns out, air is pretty springy. Without enough of that springy air, an underinflated soccer ball only has one way of storing energy when it bounces. The leather surface of the ball deforms, or bends. But it's not very good at springing back into shape again, so not much of that potential energy gets turned back into kinetic energy."

"Then where does it go?" Alberta asked.

"Great question!" Mr. Flask said. "It changes into another kind of energy — heat. Actually, even the bounciest ball loses some energy to heat with each bounce. That's one reason why no ball bounces forever."

Heather looked back down at her soccer ball.

"Wait! Why is it even important how well a soccer ball bounces? It's not like it's a basketball."

"Another great question," the teacher said. "When you look at it from a physics point of view, it turns out that kicking a ball is basically the same as bouncing it. Essentially, you're bouncing the ball off your moving foot. So a ball that bounces well will also travel far when you kick it."

Mr. Flask walked over to his storage chest. "Here, let's stop talking for a while and start bouncing. Try out some of these different balls. The tennis balls have air in them, like soccer balls. The Super Balls are solid, like the pinky balls, but the material they're made of is different. Come up with your own investigations, and we'll share the results later."

Soon, balls were bouncing off every hard surface in the classroom — walls, desks, the floor, the ceiling.

Sean grabbed one ball of each type. "It's smack-down time! I'm going to have a championship bouncing match."

Alberta took two tennis balls. "Will two balls of the same type always be equally bouncy?"

Luis bounced a Super Ball experimentally. "Can a ball ever bounce higher than the spot you drop it from?"

Prescott chose a pinky ball. "What if you *throw* it down instead?"

Max had his back to the group. "Why can't Professor von Offel catch a Super Ball?"

"Uh-oh," Prescott breathed. He turned around. In

the back of the class, the professor was giddily chasing a bouncing Super Ball. Each time he got close enough to pounce on it, it literally slipped *through* his fingers. Finally, Atom snapped it up in his beak and placed it in Professor von Offel's palm. The professor giggled and launched the ball again.

"It's bouncing right through his hand!" Max said. "Mr. Fla —"

Prescott clapped a hand over Max's mouth. "Don't be silly. The professor's just old, that's all. His reflexes are shot. We can't expect him to do the things we take for granted, like catching a tiny little ball."

"Oh, yeah? I'd say he's performed pretty well this week." Max counted on his fingers. "First, he aced the dynamic balance test. Second, he was easily able to do that impossible balance thing where we stood against the wall. Third, we both saw him slide *up* a slide. I would say he's in fine physical shape — except, of course, for the fact that he's a ghost!"

The professor was flushed with excitement. "Flask, this material is remarkable. They didn't have it in my day."

The teacher smiled. "Well, I'm glad you're getting acquainted with it! Super Balls are one of my favorite toys."

Max ran to Mr. Flask's side. "But that ball is rubber! It's impossible that there was no rubber when he was young. *Unless* he's a lot older than he looks — I'd say maybe a hundred years older?"

47

The teacher laughed. "Max, synthetic rubber *has* been around for a long time, natural rubber for eons. But the rubber in Super Balls wasn't invented until the 1960s. I'm sure all the professor meant was that Super Balls weren't around when he was a kid."

Max frowned. "Maybe," he mumbled. "But maybe not."

The bell rang.

"Have a good weekend, everyone," Mr. Flask said. "And I'll see a lot of you tomorrow at the big game."

"Ahem," the professor coughed. "Wasn't there some news you wanted to share with the youngsters, Flask?"

"Thank you, Professor." Mr. Flask held up a hand to quiet the room. "Professor von Offel has requested, um, *volunteered* to join the team tomorrow as an assistant coach."

"What?" Alberta mouthed.

Prescott glanced over his shoulder at Max, who was eyeing the professor suspiciously. "So much for having a few days without Professor Loose Cannon and Max Hoof, Boy Detective," he muttered.

Luis sank into his seat. "The team is definitely doomed now."

Mr. Flask gave the lab assistants a warning look. "As I said to the professor, we appreciate that he's taking such an interest in our school's athletic teams." He turned to face the older man. "I bet you were quite a soccer player in your — your youth."

The professor grinned cheerfully. "Not a chance. Never even seen the game played." He gathered up his papers and left the room, Atom fluttering behind.

The lab assistants converged on Mr. Flask.

"How could you tell him yes?" Alberta said.

"How could I tell him no? It's one of the first times he's expressed a real interest in what goes on here at Einstein." The teacher shrugged. "Anyway, it's no big deal. The professor will sit on the bench. Maybe he'll wear a team jersey. I bet we won't even know he's there. I mean, what harm can he do?"

CHAPTER 6

A "von Awful" Cheat

Prescott tore across the school yard, his duffel bag slung over one shoulder. He stopped short at the bench, where Alberta and Luis, wearing their red team jerseys, sat staring at the ground.

"I thought I was going to miss the kickoff," Prescott panted. "But I just passed the Strikers getting out of their bus. All I need is a moment to catch my breath and —"

Luis didn't even look up. "We're totally doomed," he groaned.

"Hey, I'm only a little late," Prescott said.

"Yeah, but you're not the only one," Alberta said.

Prescott looked around. "There's Heather, Sean, and everyone else. Even Max. Who's missing?"

"Mr. Flask," Alberta said miserably.

"Oh, man." Prescott slumped down on the bench beside them. "We probably can't even start play without a grown-up."

"It gets worse," Alberta said. "We *have* a grown-up. Remember?" She pointed to one end of the field.

Professor von Offel was cheerfully gathering the players around a large cloth bag. Atom flew in a tight circle overhead.

"But he knows nothing about the game!" Prescott said.

"Do you really think that's going to stop him?" Luis said. He struggled to his feet. "Come on. We'd better find out what he's up to."

"Buck up, children," the professor was saying when they reached him. "You may not have your science teacher today, but you still have science on your side." He opened a large cloth sack, exposing a pile of soccer shoes and shin guards.

"But we already have equipment," Max said. "My mom had to go out and buy it specially for the game."

"Those soccer shoes and shin guards are outmoded and old-fashioned!" the professor scoffed.

"Since when?" Heather asked.

"Since last night, when I invented better ones," the professor said.

With some difficulty, Luis leaned over and picked up one of the professor's soccer shoes. It had dozens of cleats on the bottom, longer than his index finger. "Does Mr. Flask know about this?" he asked.

The professor frowned. "If you had been paying proper attention in class, you would recognize that these come directly from his lessons." He sniffed. "Perhaps Flask isn't such an accomplished teacher after all."

Heather took a shoe from Luis. "It looks like we'll have to lift our feet a mile high with every step."

"You'll get used to it soon enough," the professor said. "And your effort will be quickly rewarded with a much better grip on the playing field. You don't need Mr. Flask to tell you that you'll have a distinct advantage in traction."

"What's up with the new shin guards?" Sean reached down and picked one up. "Whoa, they're heavy!"

The professor nodded. "They should be quite effective in lowering your center of gravity. And as Flask points out, the lower something's center of gravity is, the more stable it is."

Luis frowned. "Mr. Flask thinks this stuff will help our team win the game?"

"Not without this," the professor said. He reached into an old carpetbag and pulled out a ball.

"But we have our own lucky team ball," Prescott said.

"Why rely on luck, when you can rely on science?" the professor asked. "You know that Mr. Flask would agree with *that*."

Prescott nodded reluctantly.

The professor dropped his ball onto the hard-packed dirt. It hit the ground with a sharp thud and sprang back like a Super Ball. "My new design delivers much more bounce and therefore, more mileage per kick."

"But this equipment doesn't follow league regulations," Luis said. "I can't believe Mr. Flask would ask us to use it. It could get us disqualified!"

Heather nodded. "I didn't skip cheerleading all week just to get thrown out of this game."

"If we're disqualified, my mother will kill me," Max added. "Or at least withhold a few privileges."

The professor bared his teeth in a grin. "Could it be that young Flask doesn't inspire as much allegiance as it seemed? Perhaps he's neither a great teacher nor a great coach."

"That's not true," Prescott said. "We'd do anything for Mr. Flask."

"That's what I thought," the professor said. "Then it's settled. You'll use the new equipment." He closed up the bag and turned toward the referee, who was walking across the field. "I'd like to call for an equipment check!"

The ref nodded. "I don't do them very often, but it sounds appropriate for a championship game. Have to make sure everything's aboveboard, and all that." He lined the players up and checked their cleats, one by one. Then he trotted across the field to check the other team's equipment.

The professor watched him go with satisfaction. "Okay, everyone, it's time to dress for extra traction and stability." He walked from player to player, passing out his doctored cleats and shin guards.

"But the ref just checked what we already have on," Prescott said.

The professor glared at him and handed him the superlong-cleated shoes and the heavy shin guards.

Prescott looked miserably at the equipment, then sat down and started untying his soccer shoes. "I wish Mr. Flask were here. I'm sure he'd do a better job of explaining all of this." He slipped on the professor's soccer shoes and stood up.

Atom swooped down and picked up Prescott's old cleats by the laces. He carried them behind the bench and dropped them onto a growing pile.

Alberta hopped over to Prescott and leaned on her crutches. "How do they feel?"

Prescott took a few experimental steps, lifting his knees high to clear the grass. "I feel like I'm in a marching band."

The professor called the team together. "I urge you to go out there and play for the honor of science. What you prove here today could change the future of soccer equipment forever."

Heather pointed to the professor's soccer ball. "Do you really want me to take that ball out to the ref? He may not approve it as the game ball."

The professor frowned. "In that case, take your lucky ball out to him instead."

"Thank goodness," Alberta whispered to Luis. "They're going to have enough trouble as it is."

"Then as soon as you get a chance, kick the ball out-of-bounds near our bench," the professor continued. "I'll make the necessary substitution."

"Wait," Luis spoke up. "Did Mr. Flask approve that, too?"

The professor shaded his eyes with one hand and made a big show of searching the field. "If young Flask had bothered to make an appearance, we could ask him. But in his absence, I have to institute my own policies."

The professor looked around the circle of red-uniformed players, who gazed back expectantly. His expression turned impatient. "Now get out there and — do whatever you do." He stifled a yawn and wandered off toward the bench.

The players looked around, a little startled.

Alberta nudged Luis. "You're team captain. Do something!"

Luis nodded and cleared his throat. "Uh, Heather should go out for the coin toss, since I'm not playing. If you win the toss, let Sean decide which goal he wants to defend this half. The rest of you know your positions. You're great players, and you've worked hard to get to the championship. Just go out and fight fair, but hard." He paused and looked toward the parking lot. "Let's win this one for Mr. Flask — wherever he is."

The Strikers won the toss and chose possession. After the tip-off, Prescott quickly found himself in a position to intercept a pass. He took a few careful steps and stopped the ball with his knees. As it dropped, he picked up his foot and attempted a lofted instep kick. Almost instantly, his four-inch cleats caught the turf, and the ball spun out of his control — and over the touchline.

The ref's whistle sounded. "Strikers' throw-in!"

The professor pushed himself off the bench and scrambled for the ball, which had come to a stop just over the line. He turned away from the field, faking a cough. When a Striker approached for the throw-in, the professor handed her his doctored ball with a smile.

The Strikers easily kept command of the ball, moving it down the field through a maze of tripping, stumbling Aces. An Ace fullback who tripped and fell to his knees was pinned to the ground by his heavy shin guards. Prescott, through luck as much as skill, managed to steal the ball and pass it in the general direction of Heather. Using steps as precise as a ballerina's, she dribbled the ball within shooting range of the Strikers' goal. She took aim just left of the goalie and kicked hard. The ball flashed forward, striking the goal's left post and bouncing back. It sailed halfway down the field and took a single bounce off the head of the Strikers' center forward. Both teams watched dumbfounded as the supercharged ball flew right toward the Aces' goal. Prescott finally came to and positioned himself in front of the ball. He jumped to head it off track and succeeded in blasting the ball skyward. It rose 20 feet into the air, then dropped back toward the field, hitting the ground right in front of Sean. Sean launched his body toward it, but it rebounded too quickly, stretching the back of the net where it struck. Before Sean could recover, the ball bounced back out onto the field and came to a stop a few yards away from Prescott.

Both teams turned toward the ref to see how he would call this improbable goal. After a long pause, he blew his whistle. "Goal. But I want to see that ball, Aces."

Prescott drew in a deep breath. Once the ref got a good look at the professor's ball, the game would be over and the championship forfeited. He dropped his head and approached the ball to pass it to the ref. But before his boot made contact, Atom landed on the ball with talons spread. The parrot gripped the ball and took off over Prescott's head. *Bam!* The ball popped like a balloon, and Atom carried the remains above the treetops.

The ref stormed over to Professor von Offel. "You'd better have a good explanation for all of this."

The professor shrugged. "You just can't get good mascots these days."

The ref pointed to Max, who was standing on the sidelines with another substitute. "Number 9, you go after that ball."

Max stomped off. "If they'd just believed me when I said the professor was a ghost, none of this would be happening," he grumbled.

The ref spun back toward the field. "Number 7, I want to see your soccer shoes. You, too, number 11."

Prescott and Heather clomped over to the ref. He inspected their four-inch cleats and turned to the professor. "These are totally against regulations! I could have both of these players thrown off the field for the rest of the game."

The professor looked shocked. "Why didn't you say something earlier? I specifically remember an equipment check."

"These are not the same soccer shoes they were wearing earlier!" the ref said.

"Are you accusing the host team of cheating?" the professor demanded. "If so, their principal is likely to ban the soccer league from the school grounds. The youngsters of Arcana will have to turn to legitimate sports, like skittles and fox hunting."

The ref's face turned beet red. "I don't care whether they have to play tiddledywinks —"

"What's going on? Can I do anything to help?" The speaker's mountain bike sped down the path between the parking lot and the field.

"It's Mr. Flask!" Luis shouted.

The teacher dumped his bike near the bench and rushed over to the ref. He held out his hand. "I'm Ethan Flask, the Aces' coach. I'm sorry to be so late. Somehow, I locked myself in my basement."

"How odd!" the professor exclaimed.

The lab assistants shared a look.

"This championship match is over," the ref said. "I've caught your team cheating."

CHAPTER 7

He Doesn't Know His Own Strength

"Cheating?" Mr. Flask looked at his lab assistants.

"Your new equipment," Luis explained. "It didn't meet regulations."

"What new equipment?" the teacher asked.

Heather lifted a playing boot. "These high-traction cleats, and the stabilizing shin guards, and the high-bouncing ball."

The ref put his hands on his hips. "If you approved this equipment, then that settles it."

"But I *didn't* approve it," Mr. Flask said. "In fact, I have no idea where it came" — his eyes shifted to the professor — "from."

The professor sniffed. "Well, you taught those lessons on traction, balance, and bouncing balls. Then you agreed to let me act as assistant coach. One need only connect the dots to see that you were behind all this!"

Mr. Flask turned back to the ref. "I understand there have been some serious rule infractions here, but my players aren't to blame. Penalize me if you have to for my" — his eyes flicked toward the professor again — "staffing misjudgments. But please allow my players to get back into their regular gear and continue the game."

The ref frowned. "I'll have to talk it over with the Strikers' coach." He took off across the field.

The lab assistants quickly filled Mr. Flask in on the first 90 seconds of the game. The professor listened uninterestedly, then wandered back to the bench.

A few minutes later, the ref returned. "The Strikers' coach says they came here to play," he said. "He's even willing to scrub their goal and start over, but I want it to stand. I'll give you five minutes to get your players back into regulation gear."

Mr. Flask smiled. "Thank you." He waved across the field to the Strikers' coach, who held up a hand in acknowledgment.

Mr. Flask called the Aces over and quickly collected the professor's gear. As he watched the pile of doctored cleats grow, he shook his head in wonder. "Only the mind of a von Offel could cook up a plan like this."

After a second equipment check, the Aces took the field again. This time, the play was more predictable, with both Heather and the Strikers' center forward driving hard. There were about a dozen attempts but no successful goals until early in the second half, when a well-placed chip kick from Heather tied the game 1–1. The Aces went wild, and Heather grabbed

Prescott for a celebratory hug. As Prescott returned to his position for the kickoff, he was flushed with equal parts pleasure and embarrassment.

The score stayed locked well into the second half. With two minutes on the clock, both teams were hungry for a winning goal. They were also tired. Prescott found himself less surefooted than usual as he moved in to tackle one of the advancing Striker forwards. He accidentally kicked her, earning a direct free kick for the opposing team.

Sean groaned with exhaustion as the Striker forward lined up for the kick. "Prescott, you owe me a serious sugar fix for this!"

The Striker kicked, and Sean hurled himself at the ball, neatly blocking it.

"Good job, Sean!" Mr. Flask called from the sideline.

Sean threw the ball back into play.

"I found it!"

Mr. Flask spun around to see Max trudging toward him, holding a white-and-black scrap of plastic.

"The professor's ball," Max panted. He held it out to Mr. Flask.

The teacher looked at the limp scrap. "Um, good job, Max. How in the world did you find it?"

Max colored. "Well, after about an hour of searching, that stupid bird finally dropped it on my head."

"Ooooooh!" A thin wail rose from the playing field. Prescott was down on the field, clutching his leg.

A player kicked the ball out of bounds to stop play, and Mr. Flask ran out onto the field.

"I think I'm okay," Prescott told him.

"We'd better get you off the field, though." The teacher helped Prescott to the bench.

Max crowded them. "Mr. Fla-ask. *I* haven't played yet."

"Looks like you got back just in time, Max," the teacher said. "You're in at Prescott's halfback position. Just one piece of advice. If you get the ball, pass it directly to Heather."

Prescott watched Max head toward the field. He was lifting his legs in a familiar marching band way. "Wait! He's still wearing the professor's equipment!"

The teacher called Max back and helped him find his own cleats and shin guards. Max started toward the field for the second time. Now his marching steps were even higher. "Wow! My legs feel as light as air!" he said.

"This should be interesting from a scientific point of view," Mr. Flask said to Prescott. "Max has been running around for so long in those four-inch cleats that he's used to lifting his feet high, and those heavy shin guards with them. Now that his equipment is back to normal, it might take him a little while to readjust."

Play resumed with less than a minute left on the clock. Both teams were pushing hard, and ball possession seesawed back and forth as the seconds counted down. Finally, a Striker forward broke away

62

and drove the ball toward the Aces' goal. Max ran to meet him. With each step, he leaped high in the air like a bounding gazelle.

"Oh, man," Prescott said. "Maybe I should get back out there. My ankle's not that bad."

"Give Max a chance," Mr. Flask said. "You never know what'll happen on the field." Prescott looked down and noticed that the teacher's knuckles were white with tension.

The Striker forward wove around Max but ran smack into another Aces, halfback, who deftly stole the ball. Heather immediately lost the two Strikers guarding her and signaled for a pass.

As soon as she had the ball, Heather dribbled toward the Strikers' goal and kicked hard. Her aim was good, but the goalie intercepted the ball and whipped it across the field to the Striker center forward. He flew down the field toward the Aces' goal. With 10 seconds on the clock, the only two things between him and the goal were Sean and Max. And Max was frozen like a deer in headlights.

"Go for the tackle, Max!" Prescott screamed.

"You can do it!" Mr. Flask added.

Max blinked and bounded cautiously toward the Striker forward. He kept his eye on the ball, approached the forward, and poked his toe at the ball. His jaw dropped as he saw the ball actually spin out of the forward's possession and roll toward the touchline. His kick had clearly been much more powerful than he'd intended. Max took a few desperate leaps and trapped the ball under his foot. The Striker forward spun around and headed for him.

"I'm open!" Heather called. She waved her arms.

Max pulled back his foot and launched the ball toward Heather. His kick was so powerful that it shot between her arms, sailed over the heads of the Striker defense, and landed neatly in the goal.

The clock clicked to 00:00.

Max sunk to his knees. "I'm sorry, Mr. Fla-ask! I really tried to kick it to Heather."

The teacher ran out onto the field. "Don't apologize, Max," he laughed. "You just won us the championship!"

On the bench, the professor sniffed indignantly. "*He* won the championship?" he complained to Atom. "And I suppose my inventive warm-up equipment gets no credit?"

The Aces lifted Max over their heads and carried him off the field. Prescott limped over to Alberta and Luis.

Mr. Flask joined the lab assistants. "You guys played a great season. Congratulations!"

Luis nodded. "Thanks, Coach."

Alberta grinned.

"But who would have thought the championship would be determined by a lucky kick like that?" Prescott said.

"It wasn't completely luck," Mr. Flask said. "It was also science. In baseball, players warm up with an extra-heavy weighted bat. Then when they go to hit the ball with a regular bat, their muscles over-compensate, and they hit harder. The professor's heavy shin guards must have acted like a weighted bat. Max ran around in them for more than an hour. So when Max went to kick without the extra weight, his muscles overcompensated, and he kicked harder."

The professor walked over and sharply tapped Mr. Flask on the shoulder. "There's no need for a formal show of appreciation," he said. "Top billing on the championship trophy will be thanks enough for me." He shouldered his bag of equipment and began to walk away.

Mr. Flask smiled. "As I said, you never know what'll happen on the field."

Atom, riding on the professor's sack, let out a loud squawk. "At least not when a von Offel is around."

The lab assistants glared at him.

"Awk!" the parrot gulped.

Welcome to the World of
MAD SCIENCE!

The Mad Science Group has been providing live, interactive, exciting science experiences for children throughout the world for more than 12 years. Our goal is to provide children with fun, entertaining, and exciting activities that instill a clearer understanding of what science is really about and how it affects the world around them. Founded in Montreal, Canada, we currently have 125 locations throughout the world.

Our commitment to science education is demonstrated throughout this imaginative series that mixes hilarious fiction with factual information to show how science plays an important role in our daily lives. To add to the learning fun, we've also created exciting, accessible experiment logs so that children can bring the excitement of hands-on science right into their homes.

To discover more about Mad Science and how to bring our interactive science experience to your home or school, check out our website:

http://www.madscience.org

We spark the imagination and curiosity of children everywhere!